If you have never heard the story of how a regular kitty became a superhero kitty, then you will want to read on.

If you already know the story of Fashion Kitty, you might want to read on anyway, because stories about super powers are usually interesting and amazing, and these kinds of stories are fun to hear about again and again.

Fashion Kitty

AND THE

B.O.Y.S.

(Ball of Yellow String)

By Charise Mericle Harper

Disney·HYPERION BOOKS
NEW YORK

Text and illustrations copyright © 2011 by Charise Mericle Harper

Printed in Singapore
First Edition
10 9 8 7 6 5 4 3 2
F850-6835-5-11-351

Library of Congress Cataloging-in-Publication Data
Harper, Charise Mericle.
  Fashion Kitty and the B.O.Y.S. (Ball of Yellow String) / by Charise Mericle Harper. — 1st ed.
    p. cm.
  Summary: Fashion Kitty, a superhero who rescues victims from fashion emergencies, faces a new nemesis: dastardly junior inventor Leon Lambaster III and his gang, the B.O.Y.S., who are determined to capture the intrepid feline and expose her secret identity.
  ISBN 978-1-4231-3654-5
  [1. Cats—Fiction. 2. Superheroes—Fiction. 3. Fashion—Fiction.] I. Title. II. Title: Fashion Kitty and the B.O.Y.S. (Ball of Yellow String)
  PZ7.7.H37Fas 2011
  741.5'973—dc23
                  2011010702

Reinforced binding

Visit www.disneyhyperionbooks.com

This book is dedicated to
all the boys who read it.
Are you a boy?
Are you reading this?
Then that means you!
. . . And to the girls:
XO to you!!!

Chapter 1

How Kiki Kittie Became Fashion Kitty

This is Kiki Kittie.

Before Kiki Kittie became Fashion Kitty, everything in her life was *almost* normal. She went to school with her friends, lived with her mother and her father, and tried to be patient with her little sister, Lana.

But even though the Kittie family looked like regular and normal kitties on the outside, they were not. They had an important family secret. Secrets are not easy to keep, but the Kittie family knew they could never share their secret, not even with their very best friends. This was because the Kittie family loved their secret, and they did not want anyone to eat her.

The Kittie family's secret's name was Mousie, and she was a mouse.

This is what Mousie would say if she were the pet of a normal cat family.

This is what Mousie said because she was a pet of the Kittie family.

Just when the Kittie family was getting used to their one furry gray secret, something unusual happened, and they found themselves suddenly having a new and even bigger secret to keep. Surprisingly, the unusual thing happened right on Kiki's birthday. At the exact moment when Kiki was making a wish and blowing out the candles on her birthday cake, the shelf above her suddenly broke. CRASH! A stack of fashion magazines fell right on her head and knocked her to the ground.

It was a disaster.

Mother Kittie was frantic, Father Kittie was worried, Lana was splattered with frosting, and Kiki was lying very still on the floor with her eyes closed. Even Mousie was upset.

A few minutes passed, and then Kiki finally opened her eyes. Of course Mother Kittie was very relieved. "Thank goodness!" she said. But that was because she didn't know that her sweet normal Kiki Kittie had transformed into the superhero Fashion Kitty. If she had known that, she might have said something different, like, "Oh, my goodness!" instead.

I think I hear a Fashion Emergency.

Chapter 2

Being a Superhero Is Not Always Supergreat

It's not always easy to live with a superhero.

But dinner is ready! How come you always have to leave at mealtime?

Sorry! Fashion calls.

Every time Kiki changes into Fashion Kitty she flies away.

I wish Fashion Kitty would stay and play with me.

And it's not always easy to be a superhero.

Mostly superheroes are liked and appreciated.

But sometimes they are not.

A kitty with a lot of negative things to say can sometimes also be a troublemaker. Leon Lambaster the III was definitely bubbling over with trouble.

Appreciated   Not appreciated

Chapter 3

The No-Good Reason Why Leon the III Didn't Like Fashion Kitty

Leon Lambaster the III was the third Leon in the Lambaster family. Leon's grandfather was number 1, and Leon's father was number 2. Leons number 1 and 2 were both scientists and inventors. They used their inventing skills for good, and were quite famous and appreciated around town for their helpful yellow inventions. No one knew why, but yellow inventions were a Lambaster family tradition.

Unlike Leons number 1 and 2, Leon number 3 was not so much appreciated. He was sneaky, full of mischief, and very often untruthful.

Like his father and grandfather, Leon the III was full of big ideas, but Leon's ideas were not about helping other kitties. They were mostly selfish and mean-spirited.

"We can't help you build such terrible things," said Leon's father.

"You should try to be more like your brother, Lester," said his grandfather.

This was not what Leon Lambaster the III wanted to hear. Hearing this made him grumpy. In fact, his grumpiness was so great that he refused to help his family with their regular Monday night statue-building project. And even though marshmallow-statue-building was one of his favorite family activities, Leon just growled, stomped his feet, and crossed his arms. It did not help that today was his sister's turn to choose the statue topic.

"No way! Never! You have got to be kidding! Not in a million kitty years!" These were all the things Leon Lambaster the III said when his father asked him to please pass the marshmallows and a pawful of toothpicks.

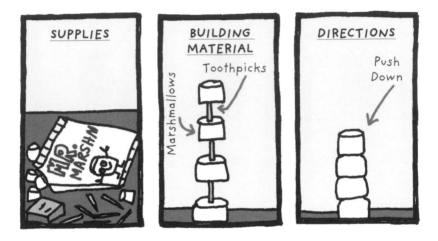

SUPPLIES

BUILDING MATERIAL

Toothpicks

Marshmallows

DIRECTIONS

Push Down

Of course Leon was sent directly to his room. But he didn't care. His room was filled with all sorts of marvelous toys, nifty gadgets, and cool gizmos—it was not a bad place to be.

But today Leon ignored all his fancy things. Instead he took out a plain pencil and notebook. He was in a perfect mood to plan something nasty. He took a deep breath, and in his most careful handwriting, wrote down three words.

This was a terrible thing to do, but still, there was one kitty who would have smiled if she had seen it. That kitty was Miss Willow, Leon's teacher, and that was because never before had Leon taken so much time with his handwriting. And in all his writing life, never before had Leon made such a beautiful *S*. It was round and swirly in all the right places. It was almost perfect.

But unfortunately, at that very moment, it was the only good thing about Leon Lambaster the III.

Chapter 4

Kiki Kittie

It was 8:15 on a Tuesday morning and Kiki was hurrying to get ready for school. Every morning she tried on outfit after outfit. It was a lot of work to find the exact right look. A great outfit had to look good and feel good. No matter how long it took, Kiki never gave up until everything was absolutely perfect. She was 100 percent committed to fashion. This drove Mother Kittie a little crazy.

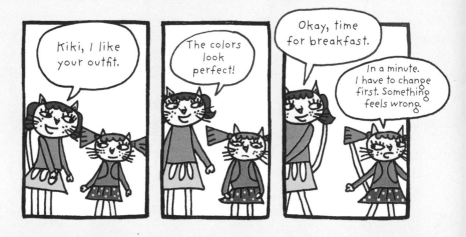

Watching Kiki try on so many outfits made Mother Kittie think about the terrible thing that had not so long ago happened at Kiki's school. And secretly she thought that maybe the terrible thing had not been quite so terrible after all.

Of course Kiki and her best friend, June, would have disagreed.

Kiki and June walked to school together every morning, and on the way, they always picked up their friend Zack. Zack waited for them on his front steps, and lately another kitty had started waiting there, too. This kitty was Lester. Kiki and June liked Lester, and that was because even though he looked just like Leon, Lester was nothing like his nasty twin brother.

Chapter 5

Lester Lambaster

Life was not easy for Lester. Even though he was a kitty full of original ideas and interesting thoughts, he hardly ever got to talk about them. Instead he spent a lot of his time saying the same three sentences over and over again. It was very annoying, and very tiring.

Lester had one big wish.

Lester had tried changing his
look, but Leon just copied him
no matter what he did.

Some boys do not care about fashion. These kinds of boys were not upset when Mrs. Rumple, the school principal, made everyone in the school wear a uniform. They were perfectly happy to wear look-alike clothing, but that was because even with the same clothes on their bodies, their heads were unique and different.

Still look different

Same clothes

But this was not the same for Lester, and he hated the uniforms.

Lester　　　　Leon

On the day that Mrs. Rumple changed her mind and said, "No more uniforms," Lester was as happy as all the girl kitties put together.

Now I can be me again!

He had lots of hopeful thoughts.

And he was right. Sometimes it did.

Chapter 6

The Six Words That Started It All

Kiki, June, Zack, and Lester were all walking through the playground. Of course they were talking about Fashion Kitty. June was worried. She was very good at worrying.

"Oh, June, Fashion Kitty cares about us. I'm sure she'll be back," said Kiki.

June flashed Kiki a "thank you for trying to cheer me up" smile. She was feeling a little better.

And then, just as they passed another little group of kitties, Lester said, "I wish Fashion Kitty was here."

It was these exact words, mixed together with some nasty thoughts, that made Leon Lambaster III say his own six words. And they were six words that had never before been said in a sentence together . . . not ever!*

* Mostly that was because one of the words was a made-up word, but in the group of kitties that heard him no one seemed to notice or care.

Chapter 7

The Club

It was too bad for Kiki and her friends that they did not hear Leon's six words. It would have saved everyone a lot of trouble. But Leon had not said them in his normal loud voice. Instead, he whispered them. It's a strange thing, but sometimes a whisper can have more power than a shout. All the kitties standing near Leon moved in closer to hear what he would say next, and it was no surprise that Leon had a lot to say.

*Big fat lie!

The kitties listened carefully to Leon, and then, after lots of talking back and forth, they decided three things.

1. They would like to see Fashion Kitty up close.
2. It would be cool to catch a superhero.
3. Leon seemed to know what he was talking about.

A fourth thing was also decided, but Leon was the only one who noticed it—thinking about it made him smile in a new and nasty way.

Leon looked around at his new little group of friends. "Let's meet here tomorrow to go over our plan," he said. The group of kitties smiled and nodded their heads. Thinking about catching a superhero is exciting business—much more exciting than schoolwork. For most of the kitties in the C.F.K. Club, it seemed like the regular school day was never going to end.

Leon Lambaster the III was not like the other kitties. He was glad to have some extra time before the next meeting. He still needed to think of the plan he had promised. Saying something and doing something are two very different things.

The doing part is usually harder and a lot more work.

EXAMPLE

Luckily for Leon, he was not a worrying kind of kitty. "Oh, I'll just think of a plan later," he said. "But what I really want to do now is design a club T-shirt!" And so he ignored his teacher's talking and got right to work.

After drawing and not paying attention for the
entire afternoon, Leon decided on two things.

Chapter 8

T Is for T-shirt

It might seem unusual, but Leon Lambaster the III wasn't the only one who was thinking about T-shirts that day. Miss Morgan, the art teacher, was thinking about them, too. She wasn't just an I-want-everyone-to-draw-on-paper kind of teacher; she was crafty, too!

Mrs. Rumple, can I use these T-shirts for an art project?

Great idea! Now we'll have more storage space.

Miss Morgan →

Mrs. Rumple (principal) ↗

Sometimes a good idea can become a great idea. This was one of those times.

Two hours later, everyone in the whole school was talking about T-shirts.

Miss Morgan was happy.

Mrs. Rumple was happy.

Mr. Chester, the librarian, was happy.

And the students were happy.

Well, most of the students were happy.

T Is for Terrific

Kiki and June couldn't wait to get started on their projects. Never before in the history of the school had there ever been a student fashion show.

And never before had there been so much
complaining about heavy backpacks.

Filled with books.

There was even one accident.

Luckily the kitty was not injured.

At least not injured on the outside.

On the way home, Kiki, June, and Lester talked nonstop about their ideas.

"I'm going to do something French," said Lester. He held up a book with pictures of the Eiffel Tower.

"Ooh la la!" said Kiki.

"*Très chic!*" said June.

"*Oui, oui!*" said Lester and they all laughed.

Lester was in such a good mood he didn't even complain once about how heavy his backpack was, and it was *très** heavy.

Why Lester's backpack was so heavy:

*Means *very* in French

Lester had a plan. And his big plan started the minute he got home.

Lester made this plan because he did not want Leon to copy his project idea.

Normally Leon would be very interested in what Lester was doing, but today was different. Leon had his own plans to think about, and he couldn't wait to get started.

T Is for Terrible

Part one of a lot going on was to check the house for yellow inventions that might work perfectly to capture a superhero. Since Leon Lambaster the I and Leon Lambaster the II were both inventors, there were a lot of inventions to look at.

Leon found lots of other things, too. Things like supersudsy soaps, rubbery rubber bands, particularly pointy pliers, big bristly brushes . . . really, the list was almost endless, and that was because the Lambaster house was filled with hundreds and hundreds of yellow inventions.

"I'm hungry!" decided Leon. "This looking around is hard work." He stomped into the kitchen to find a snack. And that's when he saw it—a yellow thing he had never noticed before.

"I wonder what it does?" said Leon. He gave it a poke.

The yellow thing did nothing.

He gave it a push.

Still, the yellow thing did nothing.

And then because Leon was more brave and curious than he was cautious, he picked up the yellow thing and plopped it on his head.

He thought for a moment and then in a soft whisper said, "I want to be invisible."

He looked down at his body. He was still there.

Leon tried again, this time a little louder.

"I command you to make me invisible!"

Still nothing.

He tried again, this time really loud.

" . . . to take my new colander off your head right this minute!" said Leon's mother. She was standing in the doorway. Her hands were on her hips, and she was not happy.

← Angry arms

"Oh," said Leon. "So that's why it didn't do anything."

He took the colander off his head and tossed it onto the counter.

"Can I have a snack?"

"No!" said his mother. "You cannot have a snack. It's almost dinnertime, and now I've got to wash my colander again before I can use it. I don't know why . . ."

But Leon wasn't listening anymore; he was gone, and he was thinking his own little thoughts.

First this one

And then this one

Chapter 11

Lana

As soon as Kiki walked in the door, Lana came running over.

She was full of questions and chatter.

"What did you do at school today? Was it fun? I can't wait to go to school. Staying home is so boring."

Normally, Kiki might have said something like, "Lana you don't know how lucky you are. School is tons of work! School is not fun!" But today was different. Today she told Lana all about the school fashion show.

Mother Kittie walked into the kitchen. She was happy to see her children talking so nicely together. However, it made what she had to do next even more difficult. But she was brave, so she took a deep breath and then in her sweetest voice asked the most horrible hated after-school question.

Mother Kittie waited for what she knew would come next. She knew all of Kiki's responses by heart. The three most popular were:

Do I have to? Can I finish this first?

PLEASE! Can't I do it later?

Just a second. I promise I'll start in ten minutes.

Mother Kittie waited and squinted her eyes, but this time she was surprised by the words that came out of Kiki's mouth.

Mother Kittie and Lana looked at Kiki. They couldn't believe what they had heard. They were filled with complete disbelief.

Kiki explained her homework assignment. She used words like *exciting, fun, amazing,* and *interesting.* These words were not expected to be used in the same sentence with the word *homework.*

Some days are full of surprises. This was certainly one of them.

Chapter 12

The Non-Pest

"Can I do it too?" asked Lana. "I like fashion, and I'm really good at it." She did a twirl to show off her outfit.

On a normal day, a day not full of surprises, Kiki would have said, "Oh, Lana, you're a fashion disaster! You can't help. This is my project." But today she didn't call Lana a pest.

Today she smiled and said, "Sure, why not? We can design T-shirts together. Go pick out a book."

"Yay!" said Lana, and she ran off to find a favorite book.

Kiki sat on the bed with Mousie and began to read.

"Squeak, squeak," said Mousie.

"You're right," said Kiki. "This is fun."

Chapter 13

Meanwhile,
in Another Part of Town

While all this was happening at Kiki's house, something very different was happening at Lester's house. At Lester's house the surprises were not the good kind.

Lester's little sister surprised Leon by telling him . . .

Leon surprised Lester by carrying something that looked awfully familiar. . . .

And Lester's dad surprised Lester's mom by telling her. . . .

After all the surprises were done, four kitties were very unhappy.

Sometimes it's a relief to see the sun fade away and the moon take over the sky—especially after a hard day.

Lester and his mother looked out the window together.

"Don't worry," she said. "Everyone has bad days. Tomorrow will be better." She struggled to get her crazy new curls under a scarf.

Lester nodded his head. He didn't say anything, but tonight the full moon looked just like the inside of a giant yellow colander. He couldn't be sure, but somehow he was worried that it was a bad sign.

Chapter 14

Back to School

"I'm almost finished!"

Those were the first words June said to Kiki when she saw her the next morning. As always they were walking to school together.

"What? Already?" Kiki couldn't believe it. "But yesterday you didn't even have an idea."

"I know," said June. "But sometimes good things happen fast. Do you want to know what I picked? Can I tell you? Can I? Can I? Can I?"

Kiki stopped in the middle of the sidewalk.

"Yes! Tell me! Please!" she said. "I'm dying to know."

It was the exact right thing for a best friend to say.

Kiki and June looked over at the interrupting kitty. He was scowling. He scowled some more when he saw them looking.

"Lester! We know it's you," laughed June. "You can't make us think you're Leon."

Lester looked disappointed. "How come nobody else can tell us apart?"

"I don't know," said Kiki, "but to me you hardly look like Leon at all."

"Thanks," said Lester, but he didn't look any happier. He took a deep breath and then, because he needed to tell someone, he told Kiki and June all about Leon taking his Eiffel Tower T-shirt idea.

This is what Kiki and June wished they could have said to Lester.

But even though they felt like saying these things they stopped themselves, because friends don't say mean things about a friend's brother—even if the brother 110 percent deserves it.

So this is what they said instead.

Knowing "what" to say, and when to say the "what" part, is a skill. Not everyone is good at it. Lucky for Lester, Kiki and June were very skilled. They said the exact right thing at the exact right time. This made a big difference.

For the rest of the walk to school, Lester felt a lot better.

Chapter 15

Lucky Leon

Lester couldn't believe how good he felt. Right at lunchtime he decided he had to say something about his happy mood out loud, so everyone else could know it too.

Lester wasn't the only one having a good day. Leon was having one as well.

He still didn't have a Catch Fashion Kitty Plan, but that didn't stop him from being excited and doing a lot of bragging.

When everyone in the group had a T-shirt, Leon held up his hands for quiet, and then he slowly and showily took off his jacket. It was a real ta-da moment!

"You can draw on yours too!" said Leon, and he proudly stuck out his kitty chest.

The little group of kitties gasped, put their paws to their mouths, and took a step back.

For a second, Leon was worried, but then one of the kitties stepped forward and said, "Where can I get a marker?"

And that was all it took. Soon, everyone was drawing and smiling and laughing. There were a lot of creative ideas.

Leon was so happy he could hardly speak, but he could think. And he had one big thought in his head.

Chapter 16

TT Is for
Terrible T-Shirts

Complete disbelief can affect not only the body, but also the brain. Sometimes, it can even cause all the words in a head to instantly and completely disappear. This is what happened to Kiki the second she saw her first C.F.K. Club T-shirt.

It didn't help that the kitty wearing the T-shirt was smiling and happy. He was feeling clever and artful, but Kiki didn't know that. To her he looked like he had just one thing on his mind.

Complete disbelief doesn't last forever. Slowly, a brain recovers. Sometimes the stage after complete disbelief is Hyperchat. Hyperchat is not mysterious or dangerous, it's just superfast talking.

It didn't take Kiki and June long to get to the Hyperchat stage.

A Sample of Hyperchat

(This conversation took 12 seconds.)

Kiki: Did you see the shirts?

June: What's it all about?

Kiki: I don't know.

June: Do you think Fashion Kitty did something bad?

Kiki: No! Absolutely not! Not in a million years.

June: Maybe someone saw her do something?

Kiki: Maybe she has a new enemy?

June: Like another superhero?

Kiki: We have to find out.

Kiki and June weren't the only ones wondering what was going on. Soon the whole school was talking about the C.F.K. Club. And even though they were probably asked a thousand times, not one single kitty in the club gave away the secret of what the letter C stood for. This was amazing and surprising.

Chapter 17

The House of Inventions

Mysteries can be fun if you don't have to wait too long to find out the ending. Mysteries that stay mysteries for a long period of time are not so fun. They are frustrating and worrisome. This is how Kiki felt at the end of the day—frustrated and worried.

Frustrated

Why can't I figure this out?

Worried

Is there a supervillain out there waiting for Fashion Kitty?

She did not feel like going to Lester's house to help him with his T-shirt project. But she was a good friend, so she followed June and Lester and tried to be helpful.

"Let's not talk about that Fashion Kitty club anymore," said Kiki. "I'm sick of thinking about it."

"Me, too," said June.

"Let's think about shirt ideas for Lester instead," said Kiki.

It was a good idea. By the time they got to Lester's front door they had already come up with eight new ideas about France.

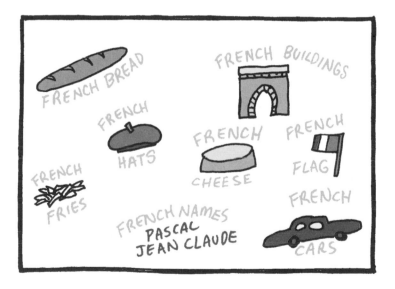

They were all good ideas, but unfortunately not one of them seemed as special as the Eiffel Tower. A large tower soaring above a city is a hard thing to beat. When they got to Lester's house, Lester held up his hands to stop them.

"Wait," said Lester. "Before we go in, I have to tell you something."

Kiki smiled. Lester's speech was helpful. Inventions were interesting, and thinking about them helped Kiki forget her own problems. She couldn't wait to see some.

When they got inside Kiki could see that Lester's warnings had been a good idea. There were yellow things everywhere.

Lester pulled on a yellow cord and immediately a basket of muffins dropped from the ceiling right into his hands.

"Muffin?" He held out the basket for Kiki and June.

"Some inventions are still getting worked on," said Lester.

"Like that one." He pointed to a ball of yellow string in a jar. Lester put on some big gloves and pulled out the string.

Lester held up a can. It had a big *6* printed on the side.

"This is the special spray that goes with the string. It makes the string feel normal and keeps it from evaporating. The six means it is supposed to last for six hours."

Lester went into a long complicated description of how the string and spray were supposed to work together, but Kiki wasn't really listening. She was looking around the room instead.

There were lots of interesting things to look at, but in the background of her thoughts she could still hear Lester.

1

Hold the string with gloves. (slimy string)

2

Knot

Tie knots in the string. Not easy to do with the big gloves.

3

Spray

Spray string with special holding spray.

4

Knot cannot come undone.

String is now **not** slimy.

Knot will stay in string until it is supposed to dissolve.

When Kiki started paying attention again Lester was just finishing up his long explanation.

"If the string invention worked I could use it to lace my shoes with a knot in the morning, spray them, and then when I got home from school six hours later my laces would automatically dissolve. I'd never ever have to untie a shoelace knot again."

"Cool," said June.

"Yeah it would be, but right now the spray stuff works for six days, not six hours. That's way too long to wear my shoes!"

"What's that?" interrupted Kiki. She pointed to a yellow-looking upside-down hat on the counter. It looked more exciting than string.

"Oh, that's nothing," said Lester. "It's my mom's second new colander, and nobody is allowed to touch it. Not even my dad."

Huh, thought Kiki. I wonder why.

Lester dropped the string on the floor and put the gloves away.

"Let's go upstairs," he said.

"You forgot the string," said June. She pointed to the ball of string on the floor.

"It's fine, said Lester. "In five minutes it'll dissolve away into nothing but a yellow splotch. I didn't spray it. Remember?"

"Oh," said June. "Well, I guess that explains all the yellow polka dots."

Chapter 18

The Big White Surprise

Lester's room was large and comfy, and Kiki was happy to see that he didn't have to share it with Leon. She was not in the mood to be bumping into Leon.

"Here are the books I read," said Lester. He dumped a large stack on the table.

"I'm sure Leon is doing something with the Eiffel Tower. I heard him talking to himself. Of course he took the best French thing for himself!" Lester looked glumly at the floor.

Kiki thought that maybe she saw a little tear, but she wasn't sure.

Halfway through the visit Lester's mom came in and offered them some snacks, but she left again quickly before anyone could really say thank you.

By the end of the visit, even though there was still a lot to do, everyone felt they had at least made a good start.

Lester walked Kiki and June to the front door.

He opened it, and there stood Leon, wearing one of his C.F.K.C. T-shirts.

Leon brushed past the little group and stomped into the house.

"I can't believe it!" said Lester. "I totally forgot to tell you about the statue. Come on. I'll show you."

Kiki and June followed Lester out to the garage.

Chapter 19

Fashion Kitty Flies Again

After a confusing day at school and a long afternoon helping Lester, Kiki was happy to be home. Lana was playing dress-up, Mother Kittie was making dinner, and Mousie was sleeping in her mousehouse.

Kiki watched Lana.

I'm glad she's finished her T-shirt, thought Kiki. I just don't have the energy for more working together.

Hmmm . . . not so easy to walk like this.

← T-shirt

And then, so no one could see her, Kiki quietly snuck up to her room.

Twenty seconds later Mother called everyone together for dinner. Five seconds after that, Kiki heard another call. This time it was a call of distress—and really it was more of a whimper.

"It's happening," thought Kiki. She felt the familiar tingle in her body. Moments later she burst into the kitchen.

"Fashion Kitty!" squealed Lana. She tried to jump up and down but tripped over the T-shirt she was wearing on her legs.

"Oomf!"

Mother Kittie ran over to help.

Fashion Kitty waved good-bye to her family and flew up into the dark blue sky.

If she had been a singing kind of kitty, she would have burst into song.

"LAAAAAAAAAA!"

That's how good it felt to have the crisp night air tickling her whiskers.

"I am about to help someone," said Fashion Kitty. Just thinking about it made her fly extra fast.

She had two thoughts about what could happen next, and both thoughts made her nervous.

Fashion Kitty looked at the house below and took a deep breath. Courage is not always instantly available. Sometimes it has to be gathered in small pieces.

A few minutes later, Fashion Kitty was on her way down to the window.

Chapter 20

A Friend in Need

Fashion Kitty stood on the ledge outside the window and looked in. It was Lester's room, and it was a mess. A large mountain of paper rose from the floor. Suddenly, like a volcano, the mountain started to shake, and then, out popped Lester's head.

"Oh, Lester," gasped Fashion Kitty. "You do need help."

Fashion Kitty tapped on the window. Papers fluttered wildly as Lester stood up and looked around. Two seconds later, he saw her.

"Wow!" shouted Lester. "I can't believe it's you!"

He rushed to the window, opened it, and stepped back so she could enter.

"Sorry!" said Lester, pointing to the papers covering the room. "If I had known you were coming, I would have cleaned up."

"Lester," said Fashion Kitty, "a kitty in need should not worry about tidiness."

"You're right," said Lester, "I am a kitty in need," and then he sank to the floor and told her all about the Eiffel Tower, the T-shirt project, and Leon.

"Why don't you do your project on the Eiffel Tower, then?" asked Fashion Kitty.

"Leon stole my idea, so now I can't do it anymore!" complained Lester.

Fashion Kitty thought about Lester's words for a second, and then she said two words that changed everything.

"Why not?"

"Because I don't want to be the same as him," said Lester.

Fashion Kitty smiled.

"Are you laughing at me?" asked Lester.

"Oh, Lester! Not at all," said Fashion Kitty. "Let me explain."

Suddenly, Lester felt like a giant lightbulb had flashed on in his brain.

And even though Lester's description was not one that Fashion Kitty would have thought of, she said, "Yes, Lester! Cheese is excellent. You are an amazing and talented cheese burrito!"

Lester smiled, and as he started to pick up all the papers, Fashion Kitty thought about something new.

And then she said . . .

Fashion Kitty walked to the window.

Lester was shocked. "What? Aren't you going to stay and help?"

"Lester, you don't need me," said Fashion Kitty. "You are one of the most creative and interesting kitties I have ever met."

"Wow!" said Lester. He blushed a little at the compliment.

Fashion Kitty waved good-bye and jumped out the window.

"Wow!" said Lester as he watched her fly away.

It was that kind of night—a Triple Wower!

Chapter 21

C Is for Catch

When the sun is shining and your insides are excited about something that is about to happen, it's hard not to think . . .

> Today is going to be a great day!

Walking to school with her friends, Kiki could tell that they thought so, too.

Lester was especially excited, and he couldn't wait to tell everyone why.

"Fashion Kitty came to see me last night. She's amazing, just like I imagined! Let me tell you what happened . . . "

He told the story of the visit over and over again.

The only time he stopped talking was when they got to school and saw the Fashion Kitty marshmallow statue sitting right at the front entrance. At that exact moment he felt pride, and somehow pride seemed better in silence.

Nothing wrecks a quiet moment of appreciation like a school bell. As soon as it rang, everyone scattered and ran to their classrooms. Lester unfortunately bumped into Leon. It was not a happy brother reunion.

"Where's your French T-shirt?" asked Lester.

"Don't worry about that!" sneered Leon. "How come you didn't tell me about Fashion Kitty? Now everyone's laughing at me because I didn't catch her. And there she was in my very own house."

"Catch her? What are you talking about?" demanded Lester.

"Never mind! I'll get her! You'll see!" Leon glared at Lester. He turned, popped a marshmallow into his mouth, mumbled something, and was gone.

Chapter 22

TT Is for
T-Shirt Trap

Lester was frantic. He needed his friends. He needed to warn them about Leon. There were kitties running everywhere, but none of the kitties running by were the ones he was looking for.

"This is impossible," said Lester. "I'll just have to find Leon myself and make sure he doesn't do something awful."

Meanwhile, Leon was doing something awful.

The pile of T-shirts being taken away by Leon

Okay, kitties, just pile your shirts here for now.

Okay, Mrs. Rumple.

Aha! Just what I need.

It wasn't long before everyone knew about the awful thing Leon had done.

It was a disaster. A Fashion Disaster! And it was exactly what Leon wanted.

Leon got straight to work on setting his trap. It was very clever, but unfortunately, it was also very evil.

LEON'S PLAN

1. Get Fashion Kitty's attention.
2. Watch her fly to the school to help with the Fashion Disaster.
3. Put the T-shirts out so she will see them and go to get them. (It's a trap!)
4. When she flies down to get the T-shirts, run out and catch her using a yellow invention.

YELLOW INVENTION

Leon went over his plan at least fifty times. He did not want to make any mistakes.

"If I know it by heart, it will work perfectly!" said Leon, and he pulled on a large pair of special gloves.

Special gloves that can hold anything sticky or slimy and not get stuck.

Chapter 23

The Trick with a French Twist

Kiki was helping June with her headband for the fashion show when she heard the cry for help. It was loud, almost a scream, but no one else seemed to notice a thing. Kiki froze.

"What's wrong?" asked June.

Kiki felt the familiar tingling in her body.

"Oh, no!" said Kiki. She knew what was about to happen. She was changing into Fashion Kitty.

It can't happen here, thought Kiki. *Not in front of June and the other kitties!*

"Bathroom break!" shouted Kiki, and she raced off to the girls' room.

"That was close," said Fashion Kitty. She gave herself a quick check in the mirror, turned around, and then flew out the window.

The cry for help was very loud and very near.

Fashion Kitty hovered above the school and looked down. With her X-ray eyes, she was able to see the problem and the solution within seconds.

What Fashion Kitty didn't see was Leon and his friends hiding behind the giant marshmallow statue.

Leon's big moment was about to happen. He watched Fashion Kitty in the sky.

"This is it," he whispered. "Watch."

And then, just as Fashion Kitty swooped down to grab the pile of T-shirts, Leon jumped out. He quickly sprayed the sticky spray onto his handmade net and got into position to throw it.

"Aha, Fashion Kitty! I've got you!" shouted Leon.

She spun around to see who was talking.

"What! Who? You do?" asked Fashion Kitty.

"Yes, I do!" shouted Leon, and then with all his strength he threw his net right at her. Fashion Kitty tried to escape, but she was trapped, stuck against the school in a web of sticky string that looked surprisingly like the Eiffel Tower.

Supersticky spray.

Pile of T-shirts not even touched by the net.

"Hey . . . How do you know me?" asked Leon.

He was surprised that Fashion Kitty knew his name. He hadn't expected that.

Suddenly he was nervous. He fumbled with his gloves. His paws felt itchy. He fumbled some more. And then, as if it were all in slow motion, he watched the gloves fall to the ground and tip over the spray can that was resting by his feet. Slowly, the can started to roll away. Leon lunged, but he was too late. He grabbed a handful of yellow string by mistake.

"Not good," he muttered to himself.

He tried to look calm and in charge, but anyone watching could see that he wasn't.

"Grab the can! Spray her with it!" yelled Leon. "Do it now before it's too late!"

Leon pointed to the can on the ground. He gestured wildly as he tried to wipe the slimy string off his paws.

Leon pointed to the can on the ground. He gestured wildly as he tried to wipe the slimy string off his paws. Nobody moved.

"Don't do it!" yelled a voice. It was Lester. He was frantic, he was worried, and he knew that one of two things was about to happen. One was good and one was bad.

T-shirt as the French flag

① GOOD
The rope net will dissolve if Leon does not spray it.

② BAD
Fashion Kitty will be stuck in the net for six days if Leon sprays it.

NO, LEON!

Don't do it!

Lester had to think fast, and he needed help. "Who can help me?" he asked. He looked at Leon's group.

"I'll do it," said a kitty in a big black hat.

"Great!" said Lester. "We have to give Fashion Kitty more time. And we can't let Leon get that spray!"

"Wait," said the kitty. "I have to tell you something first."

Quickly the kitty whispered something to Lester.

"Really?" asked Lester.

"*Yes!*" said the kitty, and she pulled off her hat. Two long braids fell out.

"Well, it's okay with me!" said Lester, and he started running.

"Right behind you," said the kitty, "and the name's Annabelle."

Lester and Annabelle ran to the marshmallow statue.

"Throw them at Leon!" yelled Lester. "Fast! Don't let him near the spray!"

Chapter 24

Fashion Kitty's Surprise

It didn't take Fashion Kitty long to understand what was happening. And even though she was stuck in the net, she used her words to help Lester and Annabelle.

The truth was that Lester's gang was not full of bad kitties—it was just full of kitties who wanted to see Fashion Kitty up close. It only took them a few seconds to decide whose side to be on.

When the top of his Eiffel Tower broke off, Lester got a new idea.

Pull back on rubber
ropes and send
marshmallows flying

It worked wonderfully.

"Hey! No fair!" yelled Leon. "Now no one's on my side."

Fashion Kitty looked at Leon and shook her head.

He was outnumbered, but still he would not give up. Leon crouched down with his back toward his attackers. He inched backward toward the can with the number 6 on it.

"I've got more tricks!" yelled Leon. "You can't stop me!"

Quickly Fashion Kitty used her X-ray eyes to see if he had more tricks in his pockets, and that's when it happened—her X-ray eyes melted the marshmallows all around Leon.

Nifty, thought Fashion Kitty. *I didn't know I could do that.*

I'm stuck!

Chapter 25

A New Club Is Formed

The extra time was just what Fashion Kitty needed.

Seconds later the yellow string started to dissolve, and she was free.

"Yay, Fashion Kitty!" shouted Annabelle.

"Thank goodness," said Lester, and he slumped down to the ground. He was exhausted.

Fashion Kitty flew over and picked up the top of Lester's Eiffel Tower.

"Let me fix this for you," said Fashion Kitty. A few seconds later she was done.

And then she had a few very special words for Lester.

Fashion Kitty looked at the awestruck group around her. They were all wearing their C.F.K.C. T-shirts.

I have to do something about this, thought Fashion Kitty.

She thought of her favorite C words. Seconds later, she had an idea.

"C.F.K.C. now stands for 'Care For Kitties Club,'" said Fashion Kitty. "Do you understand?" The kitties all nodded yes.

"And you, Annabelle, will be this week's president." She gave Annabelle a wink and a smile.

Fashion Kitty glanced over at the pile of T-shirts and pointed.

Everyone in the group ran over to pick up the T-shirts.

"We'll take these back inside," said the kitties.

"Good idea!" said Fashion Kitty.

And then she flicked her tail, spread her arms, and said, "My work here is done."

When they turned around for one last look she was gone.

Nothing but sky

Chapter 26

The Sweet Smell of Victory

Mrs. Rumple walked outside.

She was on a mission to find the missing T-shirts, but something else caught her attention instead.

"Oh, my, what's that sweet, delicious smell?" she asked.

"It's me!" said a melted white marshmallow mound.

"Is there someone under there?" asked Mrs. Rumple. The voice sounded familiar.

"Leon, is that you? Are you okay?"

Then, slowly, Mrs. Rumple looked at the mess surrounding her.

"Leon! Did you do this? Is this your work?"

The entire playground was covered with marshmallows.

Suddenly, Mrs. Rumple sounded more angry than worried.

Leon didn't say anything. *Maybe I can escape*, he thought. *I'll eat my way out*, and then, because he couldn't think of anything better to do, Leon started chewing.

Epilogue

Because it's nice to know how everything turns out

The fashion show was a great success, and it was no surprise that once everyone had finished talking, Lester was something of a school celebrity. It's not every day that a regular kitty gets called a hero by an actual superhero.

Leon did not eat his way out of the marshmallow mountain. Instead he got a tummy ache, and into trouble, both at the same time.

It was discovered that the yellow string was not only supersticky, it was also superstaining.

There was absolutely no way to wash the color off, no matter how hard you tried.

This made Lester very happy.

This made Kiki only slightly unhappy.

Kiki's scarf started a fashion trend.

But best of all, the adventure gave the members of a new kitty club a special and memorable place to meet. The yellow string had stained the side of the school with a perfect outline of Leon's Eiffel Tower and Fashion Kitty's body. And not surprisingly, this made everyone very happy.

CREATIVE IDEAS FOR CRAFTY KITTIES

Ask for help from a grown-up!

Souvenir T-shirt

T is for terrific.

Did you ever read a good book that was set somewhere you have never been? Well, why not create your very own souvenir T-shirt from your reading trip?

June says:

I have never been to Hawaii.

But I read a great book about a Hawaiian girl.

I loved it.

Here are some fun decoration ideas:
(Use fabric markers or fabric paint.)

Lots of fun images

One favorite thing

Words and pictures

Make a SKETCHBOOK cover!

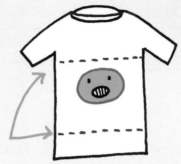

Cut through both sides of the T-shirt along the dotted line.

Now you have a T-shirt tube.

Cut open your tube on one side. Open your T-shirt.

Open your sketchbook face down. Cut T-shirt to fit.

Attach T-shirt to cover of sketchbook. (Use strong glue.)

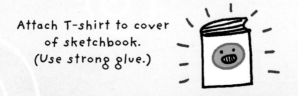

Supersnacks

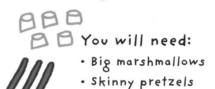

You will need:
- Big marshmallows
- Skinny pretzels

1 Make your own *INITIAL!*

Example: R

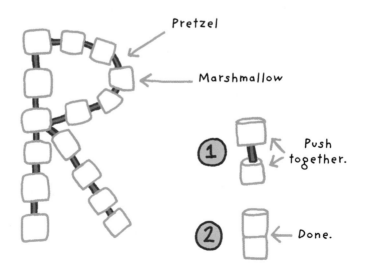

Pretzel

Marshmallow

① Push together.

② Done.

2 BUILD something!

Example: Love statue

Heart on top

Really stands up

4 legs

Make your own designs, too.

String Bracelet

Celebrate reading by wearing a yellow Fashion Kitty Club bracelet.

I read *Fashion Kitty and the B.O.Y.S.*, and now I'm wearing my yellow bracelet to show everybody how much I loved it!

You will need:
- White cotton string
- Yellow nonwashable marker

① Color the string with the yellow marker.

← 3 strands

← Tie end.

② Tie end. Braid strands together.

③ Wrap around wrist—not too tight! Tie ends together. Enjoy!

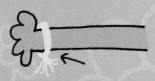